love, Mouserella

David Ezra Stein

Good-bye, dear.

I'll miss you.

Nancy Paulsen Books

An Imprint of Penguin Group (USA) Inc.

Nancy Paulsen Books

A division of Penguin Young Readers Group.

Published by The Penguin Group. Penguin Group (USA) Inc., 375 Hudson Street, New York, NY 10014, U.S.A.

Penguin Group (Canada), 90 Eglinton Avenue East, Suite 700, Toronto, Ontario M4P 2Y3, Canada

(a division of Pearson Penguin Canada Inc.). Penguin Books Ltd, 80 Strand, London WC2R 0RL, England.

Penguin Ireland, 25 St. Stephen's Green, Dublin 2, Ireland (a division of Penguin Books Ltd.).

Penguin Group (Australia), 250 Camberwell Road, Camberwell, Victoria 3124, Australia

(a division of Pearson Australia Group Pty Ltd).

Penguin Books India Pvt Ltd, 11 Community Centre, Panchsheel Park, New Delhi - 110 017, India.

Penguin Group (NZ), 67 Apollo Drive, Rosedale, Auckland 0632, New Zealand

(a division of Pearson New Zealand Ltd).

Penguin Books (South Africa) (Pty) Ltd, 24 Sturdee Avenue, Rosebank, Johannesburg 2196, South Africa.

Penguin Books Ltd, Registered Offices: 80 Strand, London WC2R 0RL, England.

Published simultaneously in Canada. Manufactured in China by South China Printing Co. Ltd. Design by Ryan Thomann. Text set in Okay Crayon. The art was created using watercolor, stencils, water-soluble crayon, pencil, two paws, and one brain.

Library of Congress Cataloging-in-Publication Data is available upon request. ISBN 978-0-399-25410-9
Special Markets ISBN 978-0-399-25580-9 Not for resale
10 9 8 7 6 5 4 3 2

This Imagination Library edition is published by Penguin Group (USA), a Pearson company, exclusively for Dolly Parton's Imagination Library, a not-for-profit program designed to inspire a love of reading and learning, sponsored in part by The Dollywood Foundation. Penguin's trade editions of this work are available wherever books are sold.

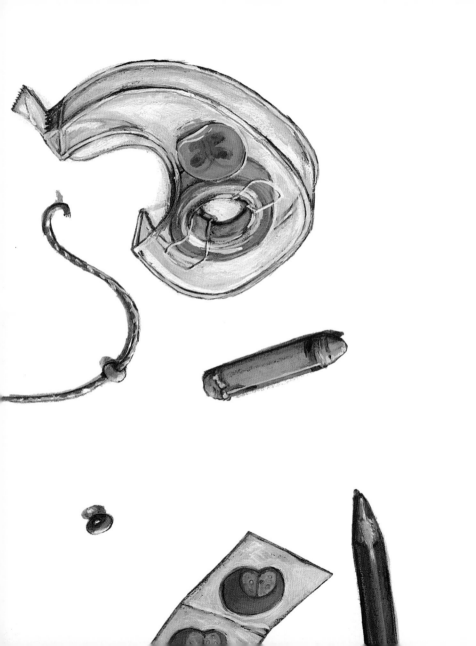

~~Deer~~ Dear Grandmouse,

Today is Thursday.
You left three days ago
and I mouse you.
Mama said, Why don't
I write you a letter
to say hello, so I am.

I don't know what to write . . .

(Sometimes I draw flowers when I'm thinking.)

Guess what?

My beaded belt is almost done now.

And my caterpillar, Willy, is a **chrysalis!**

Look! I took a picture to show you.

That is all that's new.

Willy, today

But yesterday, we went back to see that

BIG mean cat at the zoo.

I got his old whisker and

walked around with it.

ME!

ZOO

Whisker

cat

Mama

Ernie

Dadmouse

moat

I wasn't even scared
to take his picture.

Mama said the whisker probably
had **germs**, so we gave it back
to the zookeeper.

Ol' Tuna Breath

On Monday,
I finished my HUGE

wall of blocks
so Ernie can't
come on my side
of the room.

Blocks →

MAP:
ME ↑ | ERNIE

But he wouldn't let me borrow his eraser unless I knocked it down.

Ernie helped.

after

And remember that ladybug we found? . . .

I taught her
to fetch.

And that's all that happened.

Zenia

(six dots)

But I'm working on
my posture
like you showed me.

I walked across the room
with **a book** on my tail.

37 **tries** is what it took,
but I got it.

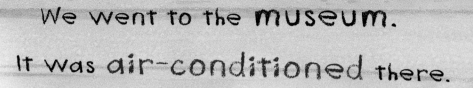

We went to the **museum.**

It was air-conditioned there.

MOUSERELLA

I drew the cave mouse with **big** claws.

I saw a grandmouse in there,
but it wasn't you.

The REAL
One!!

We ate fries in the cafeteria with squishy packs of ketchup.

I bet you don't have them in the country.

(I saved one for you.)

At the butterfly tent, I put honey from the cafeteria on my ears so butterflies would land on me.

But none did.

When **my** caterpillar,
Willy, becomes a butterfly,
I bet he'll land on me
all the time.

Honey ears

I had to wash the honey
off in the water fountain.

And that's all that happened.

But on Tuesday, there was a BLACKOUT and we had to eat ALL the ice pops from the freezer.

Dadmouse did shadow puppets. I got to hold the flashlight.

1. Put your
two fingers up

1.

2.

3.

3. It's a
bunny!

2. Add a
tail with
other paw

The blackout was beautiful because we went on the terrace and everyone on the whole street had candles.

We saw **SO** many stars,
like at **your house** in the country.

Ernie saw a **shooting** one,
but I think it was a plane.

"GaLiLeo

Today, Ernie was building a model and the glue stunk.

*Stink-o-Meter

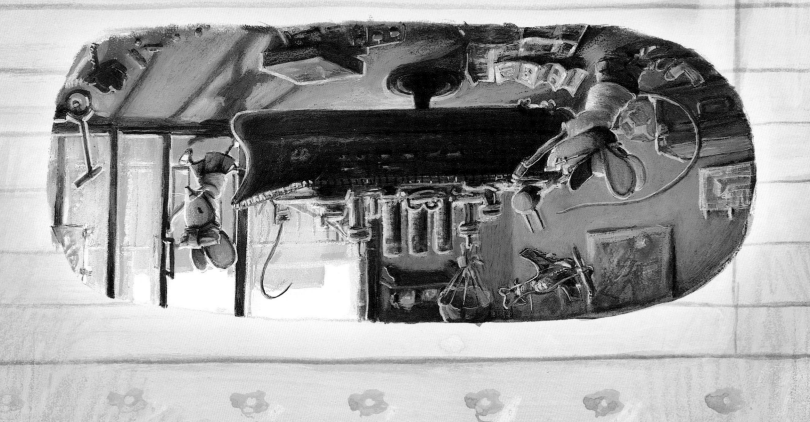

The Stinker

I mean S-T-U-N-K,

SO I went out on the terrace and made sunflower seed ~~parashoot~~ parachutes.

I was going to **test** the parachutes,
but **Mama** said **not to**,

so here I am
writing this letter.

(Besides, it started raining.)

Mama says
we won't come see you
till the leaf falls off
our oak tree,

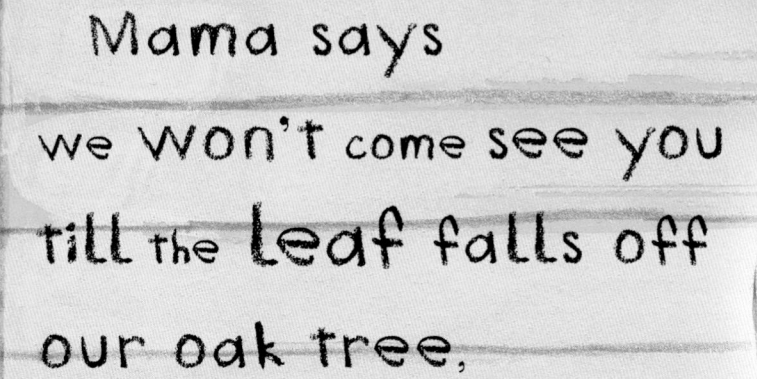

and Dadmouse goes back to work
and me and Ernie go to school . . .

After it is not
so hot anymore.

Dadmouse on vacation

I mouse you.

Write back

Thank you
for the camera.

love,
Mouserella

SMOOCH!

P.S. don't squash this
letter or you'll break
the pack of ketchup.

P.P.S. see you soon.

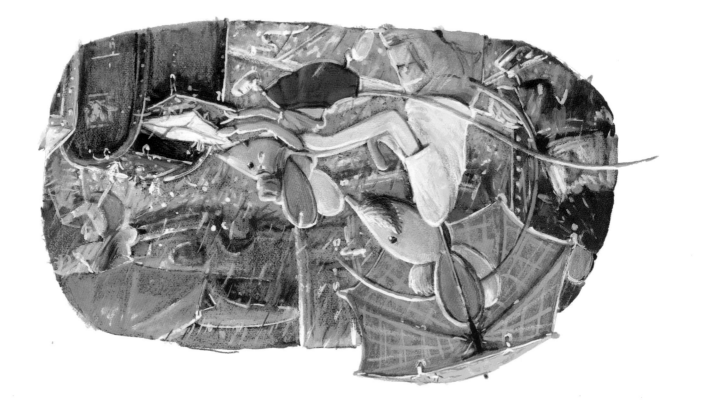